# Baby's First
# TRAIN ROBBERY

Written by
Jim Whalley

Illustrated by
Stephen Collins

BLOOMSBURY
CHILDREN'S BOOKS

SEASIDE LINE

BLOOMSBURY CHILDREN'S BOOKS
Bloomsbury Publishing Plc
50 Bedford Square, London, WC1B 3DP, UK
29 Earlsfort Terrace, Dublin 2, Ireland

BLOOMSBURY, BLOOMSBURY CHILDREN'S BOOKS and the Diana logo
are trademarks of Bloomsbury Publishing Plc
First published in Great Britain by Bloomsbury Publishing Plc

A catalogue record for this book is available from the British Library

ISBN  978 1 5266 0896 3 (HB)
ISBN  978 1 5266 0894 9 (PB)
ISBN  978 1 5266 0895 6 (eBook)

1 3 5 7 9 10 8 6 4 2

Printed and bound in China by Leo Paper Products, Heshan, Guangdong
All papers used by Bloomsbury Publishing Plc are natural,
recyclable products from wood grown in well managed forests.
The manufacturing processes conform to the environmental
regulations of the country of origin.

To find out more about our authors and books
visit www.bloomsbury.com and sign up for our newsletters

Have you got a pet at home?
Perhaps you have a few?
Baby Frank has more than that.
He's made his home a zoo.

He's woken in the morning
by the parrots round his bed.
And he doesn't get his breakfast
till the hippos have been fed.

Together with his mum and dad,
Frank works the whole day through –
brushing manes and shining hooves
and clearing monkey poo.

Zoo life can be tiring,
but Frank thinks it's the best.
Occasionally his parents
feel they'd like to have a rest.

One day after falling in a pile of yak manure,
Dad said, "We need a holiday." Frank was not so sure.

His animals all needed him – how could he go away?
Grandma said she'd watch the zoo and check it was OK.

Frank didn't want to cause a fuss, yet as he drove along,
he couldn't help but think of things that Grandma might get wrong.

Grandma was fantastic when it came to walks and knitting.
But did she have the skills required for ape- and tiger-sitting?

Ahead the sea came into view,
where Frank's mum and dad were hoping . . .

the sun and waves and beach and rides
would stop their boy from moping.

Soon Mum was building sandcastles
while Dad slept in the sun.
Frank wondered, "Do they need me here
to keep on having fun?"

So when they were both occupied
with sun-cream application.
Frank took his chance to leave a note
and go to find a station.

He saw a train and climbed aboard
and waited to go home.
But nothing seemed to happen –
he was sat there all alone.

He crawled up to the cab
to find out why it hadn't started.
Then he bumped against a lever
and at once the train departed.

Back on the beach, Frank's parents found his message in the sand.
They ran to try and stop him when they saw what he had planned.

But even though they did their best and set off at top speed,
the train was still beyond their reach – Frank had too big a lead.

As Frank steamed on towards his zoo
he started to relax.
He smiled and waved to passersby
he saw beside the tracks.

He was looking for the whistle when he found out with a frown that he couldn't reach the lever which would make the train slow down.

Meanwhile at his zoo it turned out Grandma was just fine –
together with the animals she'd had a lovely time.

They were gathered in the living room and sipping cups of tea.
Grandma passed the biscuits round and turned on the TV.

It came as quite a shock to see that Frank was on the screen.
The news said that his train was heading straight for a ravine!

Grandma knew at once exactly what she had to do.
She rode off to the rescue with a specially chosen crew.

On the train, poor Frank could see the end was getting near.
He thought that going off the edge was not a great idea.

Then up ahead upon a bridge he saw his grandma stand
and dangle down a pair of snakes she held in either hand.

She'd brought some monkeys with her
and they clambered down the snakes.
Grandma bellowed, "Lift Frank up
so he can reach the brakes."

Frank grabbed the lever with both hands
and pulled with all his might.
The wheels beneath him lurched and screeched.
He screwed his eyes shut tight.

He waited for the crash to come,
but heard his gran instead:

"That's quite enough excitement.
Let's get you home to bed."

Mum and Dad weren't far behind.
They hugged Frank with relief . . .

and promised that from now on
they would watch their baby thief.

And these days Frank is happy
when he has to leave his zoo.

Because when he goes on holiday . . .

. . . the animals come too.